To Paula

Bill White — Feb 18 1997

Little Mouse

The mouse who lived with
Henry David Thoreau
at
Walden Pond.

By
Bill Montague

Illustrated by
Maxine Payne

Edited by
Christopher Roof

Published by
The Concord MouseTrap
10 Walden Street
Concord, Massachusetts 01742
508 287-4800

ISBN Number 0-9638644-0-8

Library of Congress catalog card number
93-73231

Preface

This story was created to bring Thoreau alive for children and perhaps whet young appetites for more of his writing.

This book is based on facts from Henry David Thoreau's book *Walden* and from his Journal. The story follows his life at Walden Pond step by step in the building of his house and through the months he spent recording his thoughts. In *Walden,* under the chapter *"Brute Neighbors,"* Mr. Thoreau mentioned a mouse who became friendly with him just after he had laid down the first layer of floor boards in his little house.

I spent some time at the house site at Walden Pond and carefully measured the area around the house. I located a stump and tree where the mouse could have lived. See the map on the inside front cover.

In **Little Mouse** a few of Thoreau's interesting statements are translated into easily understood words for young readers.

Ten direct quotes from Henry Thoreau are printed in this type and are on pages: 14, 15, 16, 18, 20, 25, 30 & 31.

Who was Henry Thoreau?

Henry David Thoreau was born in Concord, Massachusetts on July 12, 1817. In his Journal he said *"I have never got over my surprise that I should have been born into the most estimable place in all the world, and just in the very nick of time, too."* He was educated in Concord schools and at Harvard College. His most famous book, **Walden,** is about the time he spent (two years and two months and two days) in a small house which he built for himself at Walden Pond in Concord, Massachusetts.

He was fond of children and would take them on trips around Concord and teach them about the wonders of the natural world – animals, birds, flowers, insects, trees – and about life as he understood it. He was on friendly terms with the other Concord authors, including Ralph Waldo Emerson, Nathaniel Hawthorne, and Louisa May Alcott. He worked as a land surveyor and also assisted with the family pencil business.

Henry Thoreau died on May 6, 1862, at the age of 44. On the day of his funeral the Concord schools were dismissed so that the children could take part. Out of respect for their friend who had died too young, they cast wildflowers on his coffin.

The eulogy was given by Emerson.

"The Country knows not yet, or in the least part, how great a son it has lost. It seems an injury that he should leave, in the midst, his broken task, which none can finish, a kind of indignity to so noble a soul that he should depart out of Nature before yet he has been really shown to his peers for what he is. But he, at least, is content. His soul was made for the noblest society; he had in a short life exhausted the capabilities of this world: wherever there is knowledge, wherever there is virtue, wherever there is beauty, he will find a home."

The following passage is from
Walden *(Brute Neighbors).*

The mice which haunted my house were not the common ones, which are said to be introduced into the country, but a wild native kind not found in the village. I sent one to a distinguished naturalist and it interested him much. When I was building, one of these had its nest underneath the house, and before I had laid the second floor, and swept out the shavings, would come out regularly at lunch time and pick up the crumbs at my feet. It probably had never seen a man before; and it soon became quite familiar, and would run over my shoes and up my clothes. It could readily ascend the sides of the room by short impulses, like a squirrel, which it resembled in its motions. At length, as I leaned with my elbow on the bench one day, it ran up my clothes, and along my sleeve, and round and round the paper which held my dinner, while I kept the latter close, and dodged and played at bo-peep with it; and when at last I held still a piece of cheese between my thumb and finger, it came and nibbled it, sitting in my hand, and afterward cleaned its face and paws, like a fly, and walked away.

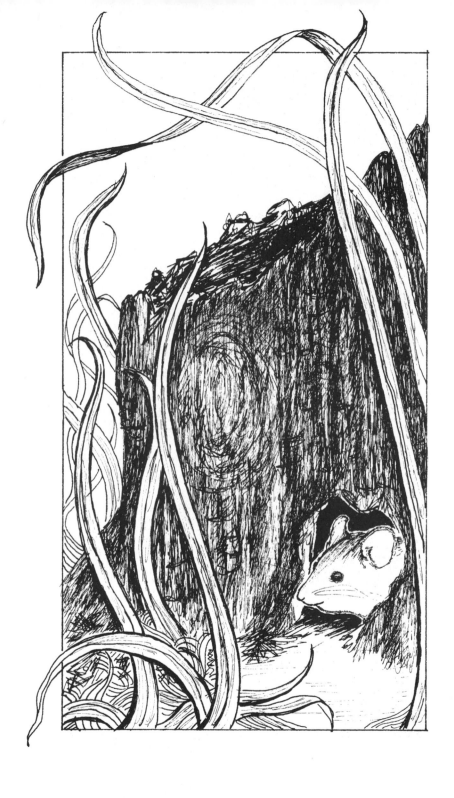

One hundred and fifty years ago, in the fall of 1844, there lived a long-eared-red-bellied field mouse with her mother and father, in the ground under an old tree stump. Her name was Little Mouse. The stump was on a tract of land owned by Ralph Waldo Emerson. It was fourteen acres in size, located on the north side of Walden Pond in Concord, Massachusetts. Mr. Emerson bought the land for conservation (meaning the land was not to be developed but kept in its natural condition).

One night when Little Mouse and her family were all out gathering nuts and berries, a great horned owl swooped down and snatched up her mother and father, leaving Little Mouse all alone in the world.

Soon after that, when she was out by herself one evening, she spotted a hole in an old oak tree about seventy-five feet south of her tree stump, closer to the pond. She climbed up to have a look.

When she reached the hole in the tree, about sixteen feet up, she looked in with caution and discovered to her surprise that it was really an empty bird's nest, one that had not been used for months.

She had always wanted to live high up in a tree, so that when she looked out her door, she could see what was going on in her neighborhood. "That's it," she said to herself. "I will convert this hole into my very own nest. This is what I have dreamed of." She started right away to think of how she would arrange everything.

The same night, after supper, she started to work on her new nest. She cleaned out all the old materials; then she found some nice fresh grass. After working for two nights, she moved in.

For the next few weeks she was busy gathering nuts and berries and storing them in her new home. She knew that winter was coming and that she would need lots of food to see her through.

Winter came, and Little Mouse was snug and warm in her new nest. She could look out even when it was snowing and see what was going on around her. Lots of snow fell that year. Little Mouse had to stay put in her tree nest.

The next spring, in March 1845, the weather was warm and most of the snow had melted. Little Mouse was lonely. She had lived all fall and winter alone. She could go out now and look for new food. She also looked for other mice in her neighborhood, but she found none.

One morning when she woke up and looked out her door, she saw a man walking down the hillside. He was the first person Little Mouse had ever seen.

He had an axe in his hand and was looking around at the trees and the pond. Soon he started to chop down a tall young pine tree. In just a short time it came down with a swoosh. He chopped off all the branches and cut the trunk into several logs. He cut more pines each day.

When he had all the logs he wanted, he started to cut them flat on one side from one end to the other. Some he cut flat on all four sides and made four-sided posts of them. Others he cut flat on two opposite sides. He cut tongues on the ends of some pieces and in other pieces he cut rectangular holes. He worked until he had all the pieces shaped the way he wanted them. It looked like a big puzzle, with all the pieces cut and notched to fit each other. They were not put together but stacked on the ground.

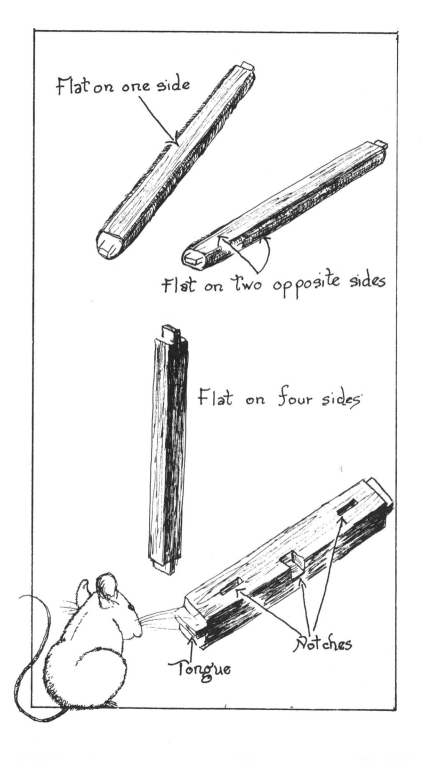

Flat on one side

Flat on two opposite sides

Flat on four sides

Tongue

Notches

Little Mouse was wondering, "What are all those pieces for? What is he doing?" Each night after dark, when the man had left for home, Little Mouse would climb down from her tree home to inspect what the man had done that day.

One morning he was late and she wondered what had happened to him. Just before lunch he arrived with a small cart loaded with boards. He spread them on the ground to dry in the sun. He made several trips after lunch. He went back and forth until he had all the boards he wanted.

When Little Mouse woke up the next day and looked out, the man was busy digging a hole where a woodchuck had once had its den. He dug for two hours and made a hole six feet by six feet and about seven feet deep.

Though the process puzzled Little Mouse, this was to be a root cellar under a small house the man was building. A root cellar is a cool place to store vegetables such as carrots and potatoes.

In the beginning of May, Little Mouse watched the man and his friends put together all the pieces he had cut so carefully. When they finished, she could see the frame of a small house. The men laughed and sang while they worked together, enjoying the challenge.

The day after the frame was completed, the man went to the pond with his cart and brought back two loads of stones, to be the base of a chimney. He put the stones inside the frame of the house on the ground towards one end. Next, she watched as he started to board in the ends and sides of the little house. He would fit each board with great care, then nail it in place. He took his time. He smiled to himself as he worked. He was in no rush to finish.

She was thinking that the new house would make a nice summer home for her. She could build a nest under the floor in one corner. She wouldn't be in the way, and she wouldn't have to climb the tree to get to her home. Perhaps she could even get to know the man and then she would have a friend at last. She was somewhat afraid, though she had no reason to be. Her parents had not taught her to be afraid of people, but then they had never seen people either.

Her parents did teach her to be afraid of the great owl, the hawk, the fox, and all the other animals that hunt mice for food. People – well, this was something new. She wondered what her parents would say if they were here. Now she faced a hard decision in her life — should she try to meet the stranger or should she stay by herself where she would be safe?

Finally, after thinking it over, Little Mouse decided that the best thing to do would be to try to meet this new person in her neighborhood.

Each night Little Mouse worked on building her nest under the floor of the house. After a few nights she had it built. The following evening she moved from her tree nest into her new home.

At noon-time the next day, when the man had just finished putting down the first layer of floor boards and was sitting in the little house having lunch, she decided to introduce herself.

Out she came! Little Mouse picked up some crumbs the man had dropped from the sandwich he was eating. When he noticed her, she introduced herself as Little Mouse. The man said, "My name is Henry Thoreau. I am a friend of the man who owns this property, where you live. I have his permission to build this house here, near the pond. However, I think that you need no such permission. You belong here, like the trees and the birds."

Each day at lunch time, Little Mouse would come out to pick up some crumbs and talk with the young man. Soon they became quite familiar with each other. She would run over his shoes and inspect them. She had never seen shoes before. She would run up his legs, clinging to his skin with her sharp claws. Then she would climb over his arm and round and round the paper that held his lunch. Mr. Thoreau would hold out some cheese in his fingers and she would nibble it. After her snack, Little Mouse would clean her face and paws like a fly and scurry back to her cool summer nest.

Mr. Thoreau told Little Mouse all about the village of Concord. He told her how people live in houses much larger than his. He described how the village had stores where the people could buy food, clothing and hardware items, or just about anything they might want.

Little Mouse asked Mr. Thoreau, "If the village is such a nice place to live, why have you come way out here to build your house?"

Mr. Thoreau replied, *"I came to the woods be-cause I wished to live deliberately, to front only the essential facts of life, and see if I could not learn what it had to teach, and not, when I came to die, discover that I had not lived."*

"But Mr. Thoreau", said Little Mouse, "I'm afraid I don't understand."

He said, "Well, perhaps I can put it another way. I came to the woods to live close to nature, much as the Indians live. I decided not to wait until I became old and ready to die, to discover that I had not tried to understand life."

Little Mouse replied, "Why didn't you say so? You know, if you are going to talk to me , you will have to use words I can understand. I didn't go to Harvard, you know!"

"I'm sorry," said Mr. Thoreau. "I do want us to understand one another. After all, if we don't, then how will we become good friends? If I use words you don't understand again, just say to me, please speak mouse."

"ok" squeaked Little Mouse.

Mr. Thoreau moved into his house on July 4, 1845, to spend the nights as well as the days there.

Little Mouse would sit sometimes and watch as Mr. Thoreau wrote in a book at his small desk. He told Little Mouse "I am writing about my life here in the woods. I call this book my journal".

Mr. Thoreau told Little Mouse, "Whenever I go to the woods I always find company. I'm never alone. If I have patience and sit very still, all the animals in the neighborhood will come out to have a look at me. They are all quite friendly."

Once in a while, Mr. Thoreau would read Little Mouse what he was writing. For instance: *"I had three chairs in my house; one for solitude, two for friendship, three for society."* He also spoke to her about truth. He wrote, *"Rather than love, than money, than fame, give me truth."*

She thought for a moment, and replied; "Then you won't mind me telling you this – do you snore! You sometimes shake the whole house, then I remember how quiet it was before you moved in!" They both had a good laugh.

Mr. Thoreau planted a large garden on the cleared land up on the hill, just to the north of his house. He planted lots of beans. He said when they were harvested he could sell them in the village. This would earn him some money to buy food and clothing with. When the beans came up he would hoe them to keep the weeds from growing. He said to Little Mouse, *"I am determined to know beans!"*

She just looked at him, saying to herself, "What in the world does that mean?"

"You see," said Mr. Thoreau, "There's a common expression that means you don't know very much. They say, 'You don't know beans.'"

"I get it!" said Little Mouse.

At night, by the light of an oil lamp, Mr. Thoreau showed Little Mouse how to sew with a needle and thread. He gave her some bits of cloth. He told her that if she could sew herself some clothes, when colder weather came they would keep her nice and warm. This interested her, because she remembered last winter when she had to stay inside all winter because of the cold weather.

On the warmest days Mr. Thoreau would take a small bucket and walk about a quarter of a mile north towards the village, to a small spring of water. He had dug the spring himself. It was a well of clear cool water. When Mr. Thoreau was getting ready to go to the spring one day, he asked Little Mouse if she would like to go along. She said, "Yes, I would, just as soon as I finish cleaning my nest. It will take only a short time."

Mr. Thoreau replied, *"The man who goes alone can start today; but he who travels with another must wait till that other is ready,* but take your time, I can wait."

When fall arrived, Mr. Thoreau decided he would build his fireplace and chimney. First he studied the craft of masonry. Then he went to work. All his bricks were second hand, and his first job was to clean off all the old mortar.

Little Mouse was excited by his work on the fireplace, for she had never seen one before. She could keep warm in her cozy nest. That was like being in bed.

"The fireplace," he told her, "will warm up the whole house, and it will be very comfortable, just like a warm day outside. I won't have to wear heavy clothes. But I will have to keep the fire going, for once the fire goes out, all the heat will escape, and in just a few hours it will be as cold inside as out."

He made his mortar from white sand which he collected from the pond shore. "On top of the fireplace is the chimney," he told her. "The chimney will carry the smoke up and outside, so the house will not fill up with smoke when there is a fire in the fireplace."

Mr. Thoreau told Little Mouse, *"The chimney is to some extent an independent structure, standing on the ground, and rising through the house to the heavens."*

After the chimney and fireplace were finished, Mr. Thoreau would light a fire in the evenings to take the chill off the air in his house. He told Little Mouse one evening as they sat by the fire, *"Fire is the most tolerable third party.* I mean that fire is the best company the two of us can have."

"Oh yes, I think so," replied Little Mouse, "It makes the house so warm and cozy."

The house had many holes in the walls between the boards, and when the wind blew, Little Mouse could feel it even inside the house. Mr. Thoreau told Little Mouse that he liked the looks of the rough brown boards. "However, when the weather grows colder, I will plaster the walls and ceiling to make it more air-tight and easier to heat during the winter."

As the weather grew colder, Mr. Thoreau shingled the house down to the ground on all four sides. He bought imperfect, sappy shingles. He had to plane their edges straight before he could use them, and this took quite a long time. It seemed to Little Mouse that Mr. Thoreau was more interested in building the house than finishing it. He seemed to enjoy everything he did.

In the root cellar that he dug before he built the house, he kept some food, for he did not have an ice box to prevent his food from spoiling. He had wooden containers of potatoes, rice, and peas, as well as a jug of molasses, some rye and Indian meal. The food would keep all winter in the cellar because it is dark and cool down in the earth, just right for storing vegetables.

When it was getting down to freezing at night, Mr. Thoreau decided it was time to plaster the inside of his house. He used small strips of wood called laths that he bought for this purpose. These laths he nailed to the wall studs leaving about a half inch between each lath. "These laths will hold the plaster," he told Little Mouse.

He went to the opposite shore of the pond in his boat and brought back some clean white sand. To the sand he added a white powder called lime that he also bought in the village.

To this mixture of lime and sand he added water, and this made a white paste called plaster.

Little Mouse watched with eyes wide open as Mr. Thoreau spread the plaster on the walls. He plastered the ceiling and then the chimney. Little Mouse said, "I'm afraid to stand still, you might plaster me!"

When Mr. Thoreau was done, the whole house took on a different look – all white. But it was warmer already, without the wind blowing through all those cracks.

Now that the house was finally finished for winter, Mr. Thoreau could spend more time writing. After all, this was his purpose in living at Walden Pond in the first place.

When he was tired of writing, he would play on his flute in the homey little house. Little Mouse had a favorite tune. Whenever Mr. Thoreau played it, she would come out and listen. When he changed tunes, she would go back to her nest, but never for long.

Little Mouse kept busy by making clothes to keep herself warm when she went outside on cold days, just as Mr. Thoreau had suggested.

The pond was starting to freeze over. When the ice around the edges was about an inch thick, Mr. Thoreau showed Little Mouse how you could lie down on the ice near shore and study the bottom of the pond. It was like looking through the glass window of a house, it was so clear. They could see small bubbles floating up, only to be trapped by the ice on the surface. On December 22, 1845, the pond froze over completely. Mr. Thoreau wrote this fact   down in his journal.

Mr. Thoreau loved to skate, and he was a good skater. He made some skates for Little Mouse by hammering some nails flat and turning up one end. Little Mouse was so excited she worked all evening making herself a skating outfit.

The next day they went to the pond, which had a thick cover of ice. Little Mouse wore her new skating outfit, with a scarf around her neck and a matching cap. She also wore a little pillow tied to her rump, just in case she fell down. . Mr. Thoreau and Little Mouse skated all afternoon. By the end of the day, she no longer needed the pillow.

As they were taking off their skates, Mr. Thoreau said to Little Mouse, *"For years I was a self-appointed inspector of snow-storms and rainstorms and did my duty faithfully."*

Little Mouse laughed, then she said, "I guess I was also. Every time it snowed, I always liked to watch the snow come down and the drifts pile up on the ground. That is why I wanted to live in a tree, so I could watch it snow. When you live in the ground the snow covers you over right away."

Christmas was only two days away, so Mr. Thoreau told her about Santa Claus. He explained how he comes on Christmas Eve to visit each child's house and leaves a present if the child has been good all year long, and coal if he or she has been bad. "Each child hangs a stocking by the fireplace or by the stove in the living room." Mr. Thoreau described how Santa is dressed in a red suit trimmed in white. "He has a long white beard and a bright red cap, also trimmed in white. He carries a large sack, to hold all his presents."

The next day Little Mouse was busy sewing herself a Santa costume, to surprise Mr. Thoreau on Christmas Eve. She knew the real Santa would not be coming because there were no children here for him to visit by the pond. So, she would just have to play Santa for Mr. Thoreau. She worked on her Santa suit all day long. She even found some cotton and made herself a white beard. She sewed together a large brown sack to carry her presents. Most of her presents would be nuts and berries from the woods. She had a small candy cane Mr. Thoreau had given her earlier which she planned to give back, as well as the nuts and berries.

Tonight was Christmas Eve, and after supper she hustled about getting dressed and preparing her little presents. In a short time she was ready. Mr. Thoreau was sitting at his desk writing in his journal. Suddenly she popped out on his desk with a joyous "Squeak!!!" Mr. Thoreau was so surprised to see her in her new Santa outfit with her little sack and white beard, that he just couldn't believe his eyes!

That evening was beautiful. They exchanged presents and spent several hours talking by the fire. By the time they went to bed it was after midnight. Mr. Thoreau, knowing Little Mouse loved to sew, gave her some more scraps of material to use for making her tiny clothes.

Little Mouse liked having things to do during the day. She continued to sew herself more clothes. She made herself some pants with matching suspenders. Then she made a sweater, and matching cap with a tassel on top and two holes for her ears to come thrugh, so that she could hear better. (Her first cap had had ear flaps and she couldn't hear very well.)

Mr. Thoreau had a pair of snowshoes to get around with when the snow was very deep. The snowshoes were large and spread his weight out over the snow, to keep him from sinking in. Without his snowshoes, he could sink right down to his waist in deep snow, and he could hardly walk at all. He made Little Mouse a small pair of snowshoes from parts of a pine cone, so she could walk on top of the deep, powdery snow.

The most exciting time at the pond that winter was when one hundred men came to Walden Pond to cut ice. They had sleds pulled by teams of horses, and they had ice saws and other tools for cutting and moving ice. They cut big blocks of ice and stacked it every day. Once a man slipped into the freezing cold water and Mr. Thoreau took him into his house and helped him warm up by the fire.

The ice-cutters hauled some of the ice away, but most of it was stacked in a huge pile and covered with straw, and a roof was put on top. They said that this pile would last for years. Little Mouse listened as one of the men told Mr. Thoreau that they had some ice in an ice house at Fresh Pond, in Cambridge, that was five years old and was as good as ever.

Little Mouse had not known that people used ice to keep their food cold in an ice box, but it sounded like a good idea to her.

Spring was now approaching. Soon it would be one year since Little Mouse had first seen Mr. Thoreau walking down the hill towards her tree nest.

Looking back over their first year together, Mr. Thoreau told Little Mouse that he had already learned one thing from his experiment. He said:

"If one advances confidently in the direction of his dreams, and endeavors to live the life which he has imagined, he will meet with a success unexpected in common hours."

Little Mouse said "Please speak Mouse".

Mr. Thoreau smiled. "If you try to live the life that you've dreamed of, you will be surprised at your own success."

"That's better," said Little Mouse, "Now that I can understand. Well, I never dreamed of the life I am now living.

"Thanks to you, I now have things I never new of before." Little Mouse said. "You see, I was living all alone up in my old tree when you came along. I didn't know about clothes, fireplaces, warm houses, ice skating, snowshoeing, and most of all people. People are not so bad when you get to know them."

"That's right", said Mr. Thoreau. "Once you know someone and try to understand him, it's hard to dislike him."

Mr. Thoreau said that he learned that living alone in the woods is not really living alone. "Here there are friends all around me. The birds and animals, plants and trees, and all of Mother Nature's children are my companions."

Mr. Thoreau played his flute for a few minutes, then, gazing thoughtfully at his tiny friend, he said, *"Nothing is so much to be feared as fear.* Fear holds us back in our lives and cripples us. Once we overcome fear we are on our way. At first, you were afraid to come down from your tree to meet me. However, now that we have become friends, you no longer have that fear. You wonder why you were afraid in the first place."

"That's true" said Little Mouse.

Late in August of the following year, Ralph Waldo Emerson, Mr. Thoreau's village friend, was leaving to go to Europe for a year. He asked Mr. Thoreau if he would like to live in his home while he was away and act as caretaker for him and his family. Mr. Thoreau liked the idea and told Little Mouse. He invited her to come with him to the village. She asked, "What if I don't like the village? Will I be able to come back to Walden?"

Mr. Thoreau assured her that if she didn't like it in the village he would bring her back.

"In that case." said Little Mouse, "I will go with you." She was very excited about going to the village. She decided she would make herself a new outfit for the occasion. Mr. Thoreau even showed her how to weave a straw hat and a basket.

On Sept. 6, 1847, they both left Walden for the village of Concord. Mr. Thoreau carried Little Mouse on his shoulder and pointed out places of interest along the way. They came to Brister's Hill and the mossy spring which supplied cool water on hot summer days. Next they came to Virginia Road Mr. Thoreau pointed out his grandmother's house where he was born.

Finally they reached the large white house of Ralph Waldo Emerson. It was near the intersection of Lexington Road and Cambridge Turnpike. Little Mouse was surprised to see such a big house. Mr. Thoreau carried her inside and introduced her to the Emerson children. The oldest was Ellen, who was eight. Next was Edith, who was six. Finally there was Edward, who was only three.

The children were all excited to meet Little Mouse, Mr. Thoreau's friend. They had heard so much about her.

The children showed Little Mouse the house, with all its rooms. At the head of the stairs to the second floor was the room in which Mr. Thoreau slept whenever he stayed with the Emerson family. Little Mouse remarked, "This is just the same size as your little house at Walden Pond."

In the Nursery was the nicest doll house. Little Mouse liked this best of all, for all the furniture was just her size. Ellen said to her, "You can sleep here if you like."

Little Mouse remarked, "I have never seen such luxury." She thought to herself, there is so much furniture. One bed and a chair is all I need.

Each day Little Mouse would tell the children of her adventures at Walden Pond with Mr. Thoreau. The children listened with great interest, as she told them about skating and showshoeing and about the men who came to cut the ice. Edith said, "I wish I could live at Walden Pond with you and Mr. Thoreau."

On long winter evenings, while they all sat together by the fireplace, Mr. Thoreau would tell the children and Little Mouse stories. He told them of the strange adventures of his childhood, or more often of squirrels, muskrats, hawks, and the duel of the mud-turtles in the river, and the great battle of the red and black ants. Because his stories were from his own experiences, they were all the more real. He would make pencils and knives disappear and reappear from the childrens noses and ears. Often he would use a copper warming-pan to make popcorn. He would hold the pan over the fire and shake it steadily. In a short time he would open it and white blossoms of popcorn would spill out. In later years the children said, "He was to us the best kind of an older brother."

When spring arrived once more and all the snow had melted, Little Mouse was anxious to return to Walden Pond. So in the middle of April, 1848, she said good-bye to the Emerson family and Mr. Thoreau carried her back to her nest under his little house in the woods.

It wasn't long before Little Mouse met a boy mouse. He told her he wanted to build a small house of his own. He had it all figured out, but needed some help. He was looking for just the right spot to build. Little Mouse, being familiar with the area, suggested a mound of earth just a short distance from Mr. Thoreau's house. She had always liked that spot. He agreed that it was just the place, so that's where he started. Little Mouse helped each day and soon they became good friends. They shared their dreams and hopes for the future.

Little Mouse named him Carpenter Mouse and decided he needed a pair of coveralls, a new shirt and a cap to wear. Back to sewing she went, and in a few days she had his new clothes all made.

Carpenter Mouse was so surprised to see his new outfit he had to try it on right away! She even made a pocket to hold his handkerchief. Proudly, Carpenter Mouse remarked, "These are such strong clothes, I could build ten houses before they wear out. I must be the best dressed mouse in the whole world."

In a few weeks they had the little house finished and were ready to move in. Next they decided to get married. Little Mouse was busy once again sewing their wedding clothes: a suit for Carpenter Mouse and a wedding gown for herself.

This was a big job and it took her over a week to finish. Meanwhile, Mr. Thoreau came to visit them and they told him of their plans. Little Mouse wanted to invite the Emerson children and asked if he would carry the message to them. Mr. Thoreau said that he would indeed!

When Mr. Thoreau saw the Emerson children, he told them of the news and passed on Little Mouse and Carpenter Mouse's invitation. They were all excited and wanted to go to the wedding. They asked if Mr. Thoreau would take them. He said he would be proud to take them all, when the time came.

After a few days, in late June 1848, they were married by the shore of Walden Pond. The Emerson children and Mr. Thoreau attended. They all had a wonderful time.

Now we have reached the end of this book. However, it is not the end of the story. The story has no end. It will go on as long as there are little mice and people in the world. Mice and people still get along very well and are friends with each other today as in Mr. Thoreau's time.

Good luck in your journey through life. Remember to always keep an eye out for the little mice of the world. You never know when one may choose you to be its friend and enrich your life.

Today, if you go to Walden Pond where they lived, you may see their great, great, great grandchildren running around near the area in which Mr. Thoreau had his house.

Postscript

If you plan to visit Concord, Massachusetts, bring this book along; you will find it helpful in locating the areas where Little Mouse and Mr. Thoreau lived. On the back cover you will find a map to help you locate the places listed below.

Walden Pond

Walden Pond is on Route 126 just south of Route 2. A footpath along the north shore leads to the site of Mr. Thoreau's house.

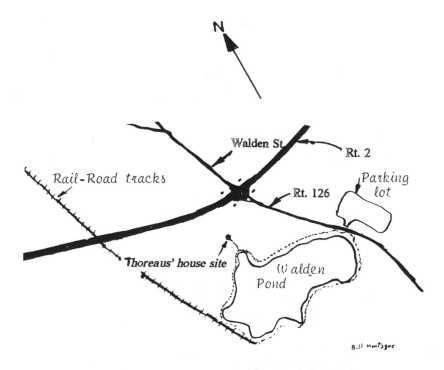

Emerson's House

This is where Little Mouse lived for one winter in 1847-48. You will find the doll house she lived in on the second floor.

Ralph Waldo Emerson Memorial House
28 Cambridge Turnpike
Concord, Mass. 01742
508 369-2236

Concord Museum

Here you will see some of Mr. Thoreau's actual furniture from his Walden home, located in a small room about the size of his house.

Concord Museum
200 Lexington Road
Concord, Mass. 01742
508 369-9609

Thoreau Lyceum

More of Mr. Thoreau's belongings and a great
deal of information about him is available from
the excellent people who run the Lyceum, and
from the large collection of books both by and
about Thoreau that are sold here. In the back yard
of the Lyceum is a replica of the Walden House.
You may step inside and see what it actually
looked like.

Thoreau Lyceum
156 Belknap Street
Concord, Mass. 01742
508 369-5912